A Bed for the
King's Daughter

Emerging Voices from the Middle East

Series Editor
Dena Afrasiabi

Other titles in this series include:
Wûf
Ghady & Rawan
Dying in a Mother Tongue
Using Life
Limbo Beirut

Stories by
SHAHLA UJAYLI

Translated by
SAWAD HUSSAIN

CENTER FOR MIDDLE EASTERN STUDIES
The University of Texas at Austin

Cover design by Sam Strohmeyer
Book design by Allen Griffith of Eye 4 Design

Library of Congress Control Number: 2020947461
ISBN: 978-1-4773-2228-4

Contents

Translator's Note

"Too short."

"Too experimental."

"Not enough sense of place."

"Not Arab enough."

These were just a few of the rejections I received from editors to whom I had pitched *A Bed for the King's Daughter*. I perhaps naively thought that this collection, which had won the coveted 2017 Al-Multaqa prize—a literary award dedicated to short-story collections written in Arabic—would be easy to place with an English-language publisher. Who wouldn't want to publish Shahla Ujayli, longlisted three times for the IPAF (International Prize for Arabic Fiction), among their stable of authors? Usually, just making the longlist is enough for an editor to make time to listen. But it almost invariably came down to this: "Short stories are just too hard to sell in today's market."

The sheen, shine and sparkle of this electric collection are found in the unsaid rather than the said, the unwritten rather than the written.

A Bed for the King's Daughter is unlike other Arabic short-story collections, which are usually centered on a single aesthetic, or firmly rooted in a particular location or span of time. While in these twenty-two very short stories, there appears the occasional Arab name or reference; the stories are not exclusively situated in the Arab world — allowing their narratives to fly wherever they wish. The narration is sparse and precise, with some stories as short as half a page.

In this collection, Shahla Ujayli has bravely and unapologetically stepped out of the trope of how Arabic literature is too often digested today. It is not an anthropological foray into the heart of Syrian life or history, though it is a 'Syrian' short story collection. It is not confined to 'women's issues,' though written by an Arab woman. Rather, the human psyche is explored; surrealism employed for social and political critique; and form is experimented with, not just with regards to length but also the very skeleton of each story. On one page you may read Socrates and Habeas conversing only to be transported to a confrontation with corporate environmental exploitation on the next.

Though there is no specific time period or location anchoring the collection — which left some editors feeling lost at sea — the empty spaces, the eeriness and the sharp irony of these pages are what will stay with you. This is a collection that will make you pause, ponder, go back and re-read. You will often be left bewildered, wondering: What just happened?

And that is the highest form of literature: not a piece of work that we easily swallow, digest, and after which we rub our bellies gleefully, but rather a body of written work that, rather than giving you the answers, elicits a gut reaction, makes you uncomfortable, puts you on edge and makes you ask (hard) questions. Just as Dena Afrasiabi, the delightful editor of this series, was able to recognize the promise of this collection, I hope that you will also go against the tide, and on a journey of discovery — of the fresh and the possible.

A Bed for the
King's Daughter

1

The Memoirs of Cinderella's Slipper

The uniformed conscript strode forth carrying a small rose velvet pillow with a woman's shoe perched atop it. The shoe was a washed-out color, bent out of shape in one part, its leather torn in another; even its heel was broken, part of its sole peeled away from the body. The obvious attempts made to restore it to its former glory had failed spectacularly. The conscript, with a group of horsemen in tow, was wandering around the city from one home to the next, searching for the woman whose foot would fit this shoe. As it turned out, said shoe belonged to a young woman in her mid-twenties, beautiful and radiant: her name was Cinderella.

A few days before, she had bought the pair from one of the stores downtown: shiny, black, rounded-toe front, high-heeled, and plain. She slipped one on her elegant foot, size thirty-seven, with great ease. It fit like a glove, as if it had been made just for her. The following day, Cinderella put on the new shoes and set out for a job interview. She had just entered the fray, when all of a sudden a group of young men clustered around her. She had a bad feeling about them. She kept her body away from any possible jab or grope, but before she could fully grasp what they were up to, one of their hands shot out towards her handbag and yanked it. The contents of her bag spilled out and when she screamed, they all made a run for it, except one of them, who stayed behind to pick up what he could of her things. Cinderella grabbed him by the collar while her shoe flew off her foot to settle in her hand. Fuming, she rained blows upon his head and body with such resolve that people had to wrench the shoe out of her hand before she went too far. When she put her shoe back on, its leather had cracked a little, its former elegance faded.

Cinderella arrived at the entrance of the office block, angry and in tears; the company's offices were on the seventh floor. In front of her she found a strange looking man waiting for the lift; overweight, in his forties, a revolting unkempt black beard. He was wearing a white *jelbab* that barely kissed his ankles, and leather thong sandals on his feet. In his hand he held a string of prayer beads. The man turned his back to her and entered the elevator, willing the doors to shut before she could join him, but she jabbed the call button and got in, clearly against his wishes. During the ascent from the ground floor to the seventh, the man glared angrily at Cinderella, then averted his eyes, muttering, "God save us." He threw her a cursory glance, raised his voice and said, "God alone is enough for me." Soon he was writhing in the tight space, hysterical, yelping, "God help us!" Confused, at a loss for words, Cinderella examined her reflection: modest, ordinary, and professional. Her uncovered head didn't make her the devil! When the elevator arrived on the seventh floor, the man was leering at her, his continued growl pushing her to do what would elicit his disapproval. Before the doors opened, she turned around and jabbed the 'ground' button, and as soon as he objected, she pulled off her shoe and attacked him with a downpour of blows. It would take a while for him to heal.

Angry and worn out, Cinderella opened the company's door. She adjusted her carefully-chosen outfit, which no longer looked as polished with the state her shoe was now in: the sides folded in on themselves, too big for her foot, no longer matching its twin on her other foot. Cinderella met the sixty-something-year-old director, known for being a member of one of the most progressive unions in the country. He started to ask some questions about her major, her experience, her current situation, how she saw the world. His questions put her at ease. She sipped coffee to the promises of a respectable and comfortable work environment, a healthy salary while, little by little, the director edged out from behind his desk to sit on a chair in front of her. And before she could even process what was happening, his hand shot out toward the lower half of her body. She reflexively swatted it away only to feel a failed pinch on her thigh. What else could she do but take off her shoe and rain blows upon the man's head, body, and face, while he yelped, crying out for help from under the sole of her shoe, whose heel was now nearly liberated from the leather body. She didn't leave him until his employees came running in to save him.

Cinderella left, frustrated and astonished at the events of her strange day. She was furious, agonizing over and lamenting a world that seemed so dark and obscure. Anxious to distance herself from people and be alone with her sorrows, she started her way back home. While passing through the public square she came across an old woman stretched out on the road, selling fresh vegetables from straw baskets to passers-by. Suddenly a luxurious black car, its windows tinted and with the national flag stuck to the back, sped towards them and screeched to a halt by the sidewalk. Another car burst onto the scene right behind it. Several bestial men blocked pedestrians from their way. They combed the area, knocking over the baskets of vegetables to allow an agile woman to descend from the car, not even bothering to turn her head to where the old woman sat brokenhearted, lamenting her loss. What else could Cinderella do but slip off that same shoe and slap the woman from the car in a surgical swat so quick that her bodyguards didn't even notice what had happened until Cinderella had already blended into the crowd.

Cinderella walked the city streets aimlessly until dark. From afar, people holding torches came into view. She followed the light to see what was happening. It led her to a large demonstration on the road that went up to the Great Palace. There were too many people to count. They chanted, cheering for the ruler, who was speaking to them from a platform amidst the amassed bodies; from a distant corner, Cinderella could make out the opposing voices of a group of youth calling for the downfall of this ruler. Before they could fully chant their slogans, Cinderella saw them turn into lifeless corpses in a pool of blood while the voice of the ruler grew louder, emitting words like freedom, justice, equality, and principles . . . .

Cinderella, now more terrified than ever, realized she had a blister on her foot, the one inside the now-shabby shoe. She ripped it off and hurled it with the little energy she had left. The shoe's body sailed through the air and landed with a thud, but the heel, which had come apart from the body once and for all, collided nail-sharp edge first into the leader's nose. He gushed blood.

As it was now the middle of the night, the clock struck twelve, and Cinderella promptly disappeared.

2

Christmas

With difficulty, the children were made to go to bed, because presents are only hidden under the pillows of those fast asleep. They nodded off; behind their eyelids flitted images of toys, clothes, vibrant colors, and the Christmas tree in the next-door room belching a cloud of warm happiness over their clean beds and innocent souls. Hundreds of their wishes swirled around with small snowflakes that had been falling endlessly for two nights straight—then travelled around the houses, soaring over the Church of the Nativity, a few meters from their home in Bethlehem, returning finally to rest in their arms.

Their pleas to their mother to let them stay up late and watch the fireworks pop in the sky fell on deaf ears. All they had to do was fall asleep and then Baba Noel would open the door at midnight and place under each pillow the Christmas present that they had prayed for. And if it was too big, he would instead slip it quietly under the bed. Then he would quickly scamper off before any of the thousands of children awaiting him sensed that he was there.

Their sleep was fitful that night. There was a loud racket, but even so, none of them dared open their eyes, afraid that Baba Noel would make a run for it.

The first rays of sunlight began to filter in through the windows. Their small hands darted back and forth under their pillows and came back empty. Baba Noel was late!

The sun rose in earnest while they lay still, afraid to open their eyes. Feelings of grief began to sink in, but they stubbornly willed them away. Their mother feigned joy on Christmas morning, her "Merry Christmas" nearly strangling her. When the children saw her, a fleeting moment was all it took for them to grow up. No tears were shed, they didn't ask about their missing presents. They raced to kiss her and wish her a merry Christmas instead.

When they went out into the neighborhood to play, they found out that Baba Noel hadn't been able to reach them. He had spent the night stuck behind the Israeli apartheid wall.

3

Um Al-Ghayth

The sheikh went on his way to the
nearby hill, remembering what the
boys and girls used to be like. On a
day like this one — lean and stingy,
where the clouds begrudge releasing
a drop to help with farming and
livestock — the youth used to gather
in the town square with family
and friends, carrying and beating
small *duf* drums or rusty tin cans,
walking behind their elders, singing
folk songs, their voices heavy with
sorrow, beseeching the sky:

> *"O Um Al-Ghayth, Rain Mother,*
> *Help us like no other*
>
> *Make wet our shepherd's wool coat*
> *Our shepherd Hasan Al-Aqra*
> *Two years now they haven't planted*
>
> *O Um Al-Ghayth, rain mother,*
> *Help us like no other."*

Their calls for help grew louder until they reached the hill itself. They threw down their simple instruments and pressed together into lines, supplicating to God with a prayer for rain. As soon as it started to drizzle, they started shouting "There is no God but God" and "My God is Great" as they scattered in the rain like prisoners surprised by their sudden freedom. They opened their small mouths to the sky — who knows, maybe some drops would fall directly onto their tongues! In that moment, the girls untied their braids and offered them to the sky, so that their locks would grow long and luscious, all the while chanting,

> *"O Rain, O disobedient one*
> *Grow my hair long*
>
> *O Rain, O disobedient one*
> *Grow my hair long"*

The young ones grew up during a time when the rain would come one year and disappear the next. The sheikh never deviated from his routine: he'd call for families and children to follow him on his way to the nearby hill, imploring God almighty to quench their thirst. But the children no longer owned *duf* drums or tin cans. Now each one would unlock their cell phone, and check the weather forecast for the upcoming hours, telling the sheikh whether or not it would rain . . . .

On the basis of the forecast du jour, the girls would decide what to wear, whether to carry an umbrella to protect their hair from getting drenched or leave it at home.

"It won't rain now for the next few days; the meteorology department announced as much, there aren't any low-pressure areas or humid winds," the younger generation said. Nevertheless, the sheikh still performed his ablution, walked on his own to the crest of the hill, offered his prayer and supplicated. He had barely made his way down the hill when Um Al-Ghayth responded favorably to his prayer.

4

Dead Man's Hand

I was driving my steel-gray Honda
Civic toward the free morning clinic
where I work. The clinic is on the
main road that goes from Na'ur to
Um Al-Basateen village. In front of
me was a white van that looked like
an ambulance, but with a green light
on the roof instead of a red one, and
large windows making up most of
the vehicle's body. Once, I drove out
in front of the van; another time it
overtook me. I wanted to edge out in
front of it, free myself of the stench
of death engulfing the road that
morning, a morning that seemed

otherwise serene. But the van's driver didn't give me a chance to do so. When it sidled up beside me at the traffic light, I turned and saw a coffin through the side glass panel. The mere difference of a meter between my beating heart and that still one; the way we each interpreted traffic laws, jolted me.

Reciting the Fatiha prayer under my breath, I looked over again. We both turned off onto the same side road to Um Al-Basateen, a narrow and quiet road. While the van was in front of me, I stared at the words written on its back door, below the glass: *O reassured soul, return to your Lord, well pleased and pleasing to him.* I looked above the words and all of a sudden a palm struck the back window. It flipped back and forth on the glass surface, clenching into a fist and then slackening. I trembled behind my steering wheel. A dead man's hand was signaling to me urgently, beckoning me.

I tried to convince myself that whoever was accompanying the body was the one who had waved at me, but I was almost certain that I couldn't see anyone in the back. The dead man persisted in showing me his palm, as if he were about to grab me by the neck or my collar. He needed help and I knew all tormented souls, kidnapped or killed, would ask the living to avenge them or reveal the murky circumstances of their death. He might even still be alive!

I followed the van when it turned off toward the cemetery. I thought perhaps the corpse could be someone from the political opposition, the security forces having tortured him to death. Or maybe he had been a soldier of the regime who was assassinated by the opposition. But I soon remembered that there wasn't a power struggle going on between those in office and the opposition here in Jordan, let alone a war!

When we reached the cemetery, the ambulance swiftly shot through the gate, the hand remaining raised all the while, pounding on the glass, as if no one else but me could see it. A woman, clad in military fatigues and a *keffiyeh*, machine gun at the ready, stopped my car.

"Where to?" she inquired.

"I want to follow the coffin."

"Women don't attend burials. It's not proper. It's strictly forbidden, actually."

I had caught sight of another woman inside, a gravedigger, emptying a grave with her shovel, wearing plastic boots, her shirt tucked into her leather belt.

"But *you're* a woman," I promptly replied. "And that grave digger over there is also a woman. I'm a doctor, so maybe you'll need me for something?"

With a sternness that kept me from needling her further, she snapped, "That woman and I are forced to do this because not many others know how. All our men died in the war, and the dead don't need doctors."

The sound of cars honking jolted me from my waking nightmare. I released my stick shift and took off. The van was nowhere to be seen. When the radio station I always listen to at eight on the dot came on, the news presenter shared that a top commander in the area had met his end in a nearby country, at the hands of two women who had lost their families in the war.

5

My Country, My Love

The terrifying news of rising fuel
prices left the villagers disoriented.
How would they be able to manage
things with winter on their doorstep
—when winter in their mountain
village meant an oppressive cold?
All they had for heating were those
small Mazut diesel heaters that had
kept them company for many long
years. As for electric heaters, not a
single one had entered their houses;
what was the point, after all, if their
electricity bill was a greater injustice
than the cruelty of nature? And that
was if there was any current flowing
to begin with!

In the wake of the unpleasant news, the Mazut heaters that had been standing in their houses since the start of the month went back into the cupboards or were sold at the scrap market to be replaced by wood heaters. No matter how much the price of wood shot up, it would never be as high as fuel, and there wasn't more of anything else in their village surrounded by forest upon forest; it was still a new idea and could warm the people for many winters.

At the wood stove and before the heater's first flames, intimacy bloomed during their days and nights, reminding them of bygone times when their elders would gather round a stove, very much like this one, swapping stories. No sooner had the villagers rejoiced than they found out that the government had outlawed logging in the surrounding forests, because it was done haphazardly and deemed harmful to nature, thus threatening environmental security and standing in the way of the head honcho's comprehensive development plan, of course.

Even so, the merciful government left open a door for warmth to enter by awarding the Baladi Habibi Company an exclusive logging concession because it held a certificate in logging without damaging nature or humans from the International Organization for Standardization. With this step, people were able to order logs by phone, which would arrive at their homes without a delivery charge. Soon though, the price of wood, compounded by tax and service charges, became more expensive than diesel.

The cold that started to gnaw at the children's bodies and the outbreak of bronchitis that killed a number of newborns, compelled the villagers to go to the nearby olive presses where they bought dirt cheap olive pomace and tossed it in their stoves, which were soon home to fragrant scarlet flames emanating an olive scent. Joy returned to the public bathhouses and the children's faces flushed red with health. When they trundled down to the presses to get their second batch of pomace, they found everything boarded up. Each had a sign saying that the sole dealer for olive pomace was now Baladi Habibi. The villagers then resorted to buying the olive pomace from grocery stores. It came pressed, wrapped and packaged in smart cans covered with the authenticity seal of Baladi Habibi, who were wary of knockoffs. One could also call for free delivery. And so, the local product's quality became superior to international products, pricier even, because the olives of that region were of a blessed kind.

When the people of the village could no longer stand the cold, they thought of the sun. Who could dare to own the sun? Before they could even concern themselves with the installation of solar panels, they received cautionary alerts that the Baladi Habibi Company held the exclusive license for sunlight.

The winter months crawled by without the villagers moving even a finger. Not a single one tried to wheel and deal to gain even a bit of warmth, which made the Baladi Habibi Company worry about the numerous exclusive licenses they had obtained. What else could they do but send delegates to houses? How else could they get an idea about those who could die from such freezing temperatures?

The delegates came back with similar reports: none of the houses were using any source of heat. The villagers had simply decided to stop feeling cold.

6

The Night the Building
Collapsed

The night the building collapsed, the woman who lived on the second floor had gone out late. She said she was going to her parents' house on the next street to get a loaf of bread. Her husband, who had to travel unexpectedly that day, couldn't bring home the usual necessities. When the woman returned at dawn, she found her home a pile of rubble, her two once-sleeping children now trapped underneath, both dead. Afterward it came out that she had been somewhere else altogether, at a man's house, the one at the end of the street.

The night the building collapsed, a man had left his office at around eleven o'clock. He didn't go home, claiming that he had a lot of work to do, the night shift or something to that effect. He let his driver go and drove himself. He stopped in front of the supermarket, bought something to eat and drink, and then left. At dawn, the civil defense men extricated the body of a high-ranking officer who had been in a young woman's home, a lady of the night living on the fourth floor.

The night the building collapsed, a mother-in-law had left her house, with her daughter in tow, to spend the night at her son's home. He lived on the third floor but was off working in another Arab country. As was her habit, whenever her daughter-in-law set off to visit her family in a nearby city, she would seize the opportunity to storm their home, inspecting, snooping, and grabbing things. That night, her daughter-in-law was summoned to identify her mother-in-law and sister-in-law, who emerged as lifeless bodies from under the concrete rubble.

The night the building collapsed, the police cordoned off the area; journalists hovered, picking up bits of news here and there; TV cameras circled; the civil defense men continued to pull bodies out of the rubble with the help of neighborhood volunteers, while ambulance sirens wailed; and victims' families mourned their losses. As they wept, a spark of hope and longing could be seen in some of their eyes; perhaps someone would be found alive.

This is what the reportage recorded the night the building in the Mukhtar neighborhood collapsed.

7

The Octopus

Mohammed Ismail was the name the occupation forces found written on the wall of the wretched room believed to be the hideout of the terrorist who had blown up an Israeli bus travelling along one of West Jerusalem's streets. Hysterical, the general ordered his soldiers to find this Mohammed Ismail and execute him immediately.

The occupation forces were baffled by the Mohammed Ismail case: his name was listed on the Fatah register, on the Hamas register, he was from Ramallah, and from Gaza, but his name was also found in the Jerusalem civil registration office just as it was in the Nablus branch. When it was clarified afterwards that an Iraqi man called Mohammed Ismail had orchestrated the terrorist attack targeting American soldiers on Saadoun Street in Baghdad, the general came to his senses. This was beyond local law enforcement's capabilities. He asked for the CIA to help search for Mohammed Ismail, who—it came to light—had slipped out to Iraq by way of Jordan, over the Syrian border.

And after a hotel in Taba housing Israeli tourists had been blown up, the local police found an Egyptian ID on site made out to one Mohammed Ismail. It went further than that, though. The peace-keeping forces in Afghanistan discovered that the house where the 9/11 masterminds had gathered was owned by an Afghani man by the name of Mohammed Ismail. Breaking news from Lebanon reported that a bomb had been found in a car parked at the Lebanese-Israeli border and that the car had been traced back to a Lebanese citizen, Mohammed Ismail. While on the hunt based on this last lead, the general discovered that the password to the computer which triggered the 9/11 attacks was none other than MOHAMMED ISMAIL. This was the very name on the ID card just found in an unaccompanied bag at the Chicago airport. At that moment, the general gave his boss an ultimatum: either he be allowed to submit his resignation or be allowed to blow up the world.

8

A Mother's Final Words

In a situation not unlike my own now, my mother had been on her deathbed, nearly more than thirty years ago in one of Damascus' hospitals; it was a warm night in April, clear skies, the stars twinkling.

We were in a room with two beds: one for her, the patient, and the other for me, her companion. My bed was extremely comfortable, assuring me of her body's ease in its final hours, because surely our beds were the same. But when she was carried off to the morgue and I slipped into her bed to scoop up the last of her familiar scent, I found the mattress extremely hard. Tears streamed down because she had spent that time on damaged springs and an uneven surface, which without a doubt must have hurt her in her sleep. And yet, she hadn't even grumbled once. When my mother felt herself entering the tunnel of her final moments, she gestured to me to come even closer to her head. I already wasn't far from it, reading the Quran aloud, perched on the edge of the bed. I scooted closer, trying not to make her feel the pain of loss and the anxiety of her going into the next phase, the unknown. She placed her feeble hand on mine, grasping the book, and gave it an excessive squeeze.

She curled her lips into an 'O'.

"Water?" I asked.

No, she responded with her finger. She had wanted to say something but all she could muster was "Ah . . . Ah . . . ."

I wanted to help her speak; I knew that one's final words are of the utmost importance. I fell silent to give her a chance to say what she wanted to, without interruptions. Having gathered up her strength, she was finally about to speak.

A cloud of butterflies flitted into the room from the open window, circling us, my eyes drawn to them. I didn't know butterflies flew around at night! When I shifted my gaze back to my mother, she had already left this world.

Those lost words were the second thing that brought me endless sorrow, after the uncomfortable bed my mother had endured with such grace. What had she wanted to say?

Given what I knew of my mother, there weren't a lot of possibilities. She wasn't a big talker, only saying what was necessary. Maybe something unknown would come to light that she hadn't dared reveal while alive. Every day I still think:

She wanted to pray for me, like she always did: May God be pleased with you!

She wanted to say that she was going away for good and that she was scared.

She wanted me to look after my siblings.

She wanted to say that she had squirreled away an inheritance for us.

She had wanted to let me know that I wasn't really her daughter and that they found me on the doorstep as a baby in a Moses basket.

She had wanted to say that my dad wasn't really my dad, and to tell me who my real father was.

She wanted to ask us to donate money for her soul's salvation, not to abandon her grave, to love and look after each other.

Not a day has gone by since her death that I don't ask myself what my mother's last wish or final confession was.

When my children gathered round my deathbed, also in a hospital but in one of Berlin's suburbs — where we migrated after the war — things weren't much different, except that my children were less resilient than I had been at the time of my mother's death, contrary to what is expected of children who have grown up in a European country and tasted the harshness of being a foreigner and a refugee.

They didn't try to hide their sadness or tears. My daughter was near-hysterical while her sister cried less noisily. My eldest son read the

Quran aloud, resting his damp palm on my head. I was hyperaware of being careful not to have any last words so my children wouldn't feel the regret that washed over me every day because I couldn't fulfill my mother's final request. Despite my anxiety about the unknown world to come, I couldn't help but compare my last moments to hers. I only had one desire left in this world, which was to know . . . .

I focused on opening my mouth and open it did. My children closed in around me, their tears and Quran recitation halting. I started to say, "Ah . . . Ah . . . ." But something clamped down on my vocal chords.

"Mama what do you want?" my daughter asked in Arabic. "Water?"

"Maybe she's cold," my son said in German.

I wanted to respond but couldn't. I departed, my soul flying through the open window, also on a warm April evening. My daughter slipped into my bed to smell what was left of me. I heard them say through their tears, "What did Mama want to say?" They started guessing: buried treasure, another father, who their real mother was . . . .

I just wanted to ask them where the butterflies had gone, the ones that should have been there to accompany my soul, just as they had my mother's.

9

Precious Stones

1. Turquoise

Whoever wears it is protected from death; it's never seen on the hand of a murder victim. I wear this most precious stone as a necklace and think every day of my death.

2. Mazen Stone

The king of the East decided not to sleep because whenever he did he had nightmares: ferocious wild monsters chasing him, blood all around him, demons fornicating with him until he was overcome with fatigue, emaciated, unable to move. The sages of the kingdom unanimously agreed that a stone in Ceylon made of black spinel, called Mazen, would most certainly chase such nightmares away. So they brought it to him, made a ring set with the stone—a well-cut gem weighing twenty grains of barley—and made him wear it. But as the nights passed, his condition got worse. The king, who was ready to give up his kingship as a ransom for peaceful sleep, asked the ruler of India and Sindh for advice. He made it clear that the king would have to abdicate, to step down altogether. On that very day, the former king slept, his dreams now rosy.

3. Berenj

It was a confusing matter. He was always seen with a black stone on his hand, its many edges sparkling. He was always staring at it, never pulling his eyes away. Afterwards it came to light that the eyesight of whoever stared at the stone grew stronger, to the extent that they could see through walls—and even the naked lady next door!

4. Red Sapphire

He was never seen without a large sapphire, not for protection from the plague, but rather because the rock rendered the wearer's needs within reach, made him appear brave and awe-inspiring to others. Nearly all his needs were fulfilled, and everyone who saw him would honor him, though his heart was so black that he would beat her. Even so, to her he was just a mouse!

10

Fainting

No one knows for sure exactly when
the new resident moved in; even the
building caretaker hadn't sensed his
presence. He was like any one of
the other residents. But what was
worth mentioning was that this
twenty-something man, well built,
classy, with an eye-catching tan, had
seduced all the ladies in the building.
They were happy to watch him in
everything he did, his comings and
goings, with great infatuation and
curiosity, each of them hoping to
catch a glimpse of his smile.

But she alone was certain that the window of passion would soon open between them, because she was the most beautiful, the most intelligent, and the closest. She lived on the floor right above him; obviously she would be the first to know him!

As such, she waited for every opportunity to gaze deeply into his eyes, a chance that cropped up only twice a day: in the wee hours when he left to walk his dog and in the evening when he would do the same. Otherwise, no one saw him; her curiosity and that of others burned all the brighter to know this young man's secret, the dog owner.

His dog looked like a police mutt: black massive eyes glittering with a beastly sheen. Often he would be stubborn, yapping away, his owner dragging him by the thick chain leash. His barking would grow louder and louder, until God willed him to be quiet and walk along.

How she loathed dogs, feared them. Actually, it was more of a full-blown phobia. While her neighbors and friends would observe, from windows and balconies, dog and owner on their daily outings, she would lie in wait to meet him face to face. But her timing was always slightly off. The elevator would take too long and she'd get down to see he'd already gone inside his home. She'd arrive there too early, having taken the stairs, and out of embarrassment would make her way back up the stairs just in time to hear his door shut. Or one of the neighbors would be going up or down in the lift and thwart her plans.

But this time she was determined to face him, to look him straight in the eye, knowing from experience that such moments take no prisoners. Charged with desire, she took the elevator to his floor just before his usual departure time. She kept the door open, still inside, waiting for him to join her. She heard him approach his front door, and her heart dropped.

SHAHLA UJAYLI

He opened his flat door and came out with his dog. The leash slipped out from his hand and the dog rushed to the elevator, whose doors shut as soon as it entered.

She was rooted to the spot, its barks mingling with her screams. Canines, a long floppy red tongue, and drool were the last things onlookers saw. Paralyzed with fear, she fainted shortly after, having been bitten on the leg.

11

An Incident in Town

In the wee hours of the morning, the town looked dreadful, pale, as if seared by a yellow wind. All of its walls were painted a mud color, as well as the shop awnings, the front doors of houses, their windows and fences. Not even the sidewalk curbs had escaped this yellowing plague.

As for the town's children, their appearances were laughable, clad in their new dull deep blue school uniform. Their town was on the edge of the desert whose sun blistered them; this was on top of their skin already being brown to begin with, so that their drab clothes made them even gloomier than before, in a way that moved the onlooker's soul to simultaneously grieve and pity their dingy childhood.

But what was even stranger was what had afflicted the town: a widespread general diarrhea. They flocked to the infirmary, the clinic, and the pharmacy. Those who headed to the city for a hospital or a doctor went through hell and back; they had to repeatedly stop on the way to answer nature's pressing call. An epidemic wasn't the cause of this diarrhea, neither germs nor the cold snap. It was castor oil. As of late, ads had been singing its high praises: it strengthens hair and nails, melts fat, smoothes out wrinkles, increases IQ, cures the common cold . . . .

To be honest, the mayor was the one behind these strange occurrences. He had taken part in a paint deal, and the mud color hadn't been selling fast enough. His son, meanwhile, had sealed a fabric deal, then strove to promote the drab pitch-black bluish color. Last, but not least, had been the deal on castor oil.

12

The Strangest Thing that Happened to me in 2010

Tell Me About Surrealism.

I had prepared an art history exam for my students: what is surrealism, its philosophy, its roots, its features, and its most important characteristics? Their answers were generally good; it was a matter of rote learning, no space for creativity. But one of the students' responses surprised me. It made me reconsider what I had read about art, literature, and criticism. The essay was something of a story, narrated by the student, wrapped up in a letter. She said:

Dear Professor,

I know the 'correct' answer here. I've memorized the whole art history textbook. But this tale of mine will present surrealism in the way of someone outside the depth of thought, not in the way of someone surrounded by it. Please allow me a moment to share with you what I can't identify as dream or reality.

I found myself wandering aimlessly in a deserted forest, unsure if it was night or day beyond its trees. Darkness cut the place off from the outside, and it was cold, a cold harsher than loss. My hair was a mess and my clothes torn — maybe a wolf had attacked me while I was in this dazed state. To a lesser degree I felt hunger, thirst, and exhaustion. I told myself this would be the last time I'd be able to keep my eyes open, because after this, I'd inevitably be dead.

At that very moment, I saw him standing in front of me, not knowing if he was real or a mirage. I took him for a tree or some sort of beast, until he reached out his hand to me. I clung to it, my nails digging into his flesh, his blood oozing out. In that moment he smiled at me, lighting up the place, the darkness of the trees lifting, pierced by a sun whose yellowish-white color I had never known, dissipating the isolation of the creatures around us. I don't know how a blue horse arrived to carry us outside of the forest. Even though my arms resembled rags, a force pulled me to the firmness of his torso, and his legs wrapped around my feeble ones like green climbing plants, and we, on horseback, became the center of the world.

Where we went and how we got out of that forest, I don't know. I found myself in a large city, full of hustle and bustle, with a river that was said to be holy. The city's people lived off the force of love alone. We entered a space resembling a spacious tent; in it were men and women, each couple sitting on a couch with tables of food and drink before them. They were charming in their laughter, their voices growing louder and then fading into the multi-screened television's songs of love and sorrow. Their clothes were simple yet bright, and before I could look at the rags on my body, my companion wrapped his wool scarf around me and, little by little, his narrow scarf widened, expanding until it concealed my nakedness. I was completely clothed in a warm sugar-colored robe. I looked at the sofa we were sitting on, and it was my very own sofa, there in a different country, faraway, the very same one, made of bamboo cane, with a long comfortable cushion, its coloring like a tiger's skin, and on its bottom half an out-of-place rusty nail.

What had brought my couch here! I had acquired it two years earlier to sit on and observe my old flame from my balcony. Well, 'old' flame ever since I took this man's hand, the forest man's hand, in mine. My old love started to fall apart, his nose dropping off, then his mouth, his eyes, his hair, his arms, until nothing remained. His limbs flew about in the wind, no longer his, and left the tent. Only the forest man remained by my side, and a feeling overcame me that I couldn't be away from him from that time on. So I sidled up to him to get more of that warm, familiar feeling, when a blazing heat suddenly erupted from his chest. I saw the flames, red and blue, then felt them, and what could I do but throw my upper body, then all of me, against him.

I slept, sleeping without knowing if I was sleeping in my dream, or sleeping while awake! When I woke up he said, "In my country, when a man loves a woman, he has to sacrifice a ram beneath her feet, grill its liver, eat from and feed her with it." But he hadn't done all this before, not because he hadn't loved, but because he was a vegetarian and the ram was like his brother. So what should he do? I pointed to

SHAHLA UJAYLI

the large, yellow roasted seed on a far-off bench on the tray of food. He looked at me. "It's called a mango," he said. I asked him to slaughter it and spill its liquid, so he did. We drank its sweet syrup. Suddenly the place emptied of its people and things, and the only thing I saw were his hands, resembling two trees, their roots, lush branches releasing the fragrance of rain in the desert.

Should I stay in their shade, I thought to myself, or leave? Where would I go anyways? And to whom? The two trees shook themselves in my face with a magical movement, making me seek shelter in their shade. I don't know who told him that I was alone, no mother, no father, no siblings, no lovers! After that I found myself on a plane that would take me back home, but before it took off, it was stopped and the pilot said that an unknown force had prevented it from flying. I knew that it was his force, and that this day that I'd spent with him was an unaccounted day of my life. I'd gotten it without my timekeeper or his knowing. We both knew that we were leaving each other, but for how long? So the next day, another plane came to take me, and I returned home, but I wasn't me. Everything around me was him; I wasn't myself. Whenever I'd take my morning walk in the park next to my house, I'd meet the man that I'd meet every day. We'd go round the inner fence but in opposite directions. I didn't know him and he didn't know me. We'd only exchange a fleeting glance when we'd cross each other. This time when he gave me the usual cursory glance, I was stunned.

It was him, the forest man himself, in workout gear, the same wool scarf wrapped round his neck. I stared at him and he started smiling joyfully, his smile slowly turning into a sweet chuckle, repeating like someone who had just had a near miss, "Alhamdulillah! Thank God!" I tried to keep it together and get to the bottom of what was happening. I looked for the two trees of his that I couldn't be wrong *about, but unfortunately for me, he was wearing white Puma sports gloves. I drew close to him, my chest filling with the smell of desert rain, and I took notice for the first time that his hair was the whitest white, silver almost. I hadn't noticed if the forest man's hair had been white as well, or maybe it had been black, or blond, or chestnut . . . .*

I got even closer, having decided to put an end to whatever I was in, whatever the losses, but he beat me to it. "I told you that we'd meet again soon, but why didn't you come yesterday?"

That's my story, professor, my story that took me out of your world. I had decided to write about it whether your exam was about Surrealism, Dadaism, or realism, and I'm ready for whatever repercussions you see fit.

I took a deep breath and thought about the mark I'd give the student, but I was so gripped by the story that I decided to reread it. I looked back down at the paper in front of me. There wasn't a single word there — it was a blank page, completely empty! I flipped through all the pages and only found other students' answers. I tried another time to recall what I could of what she had written, but my memory failed. And from that moment until today, I have been staring in vain at the white expanse of the page.

SHAHLA UJAYLI

13

Sitt Najmiyyah's House

Their childhood in the neglected quarter on the city outskirts hadn't been full of toys but, even so, they never missed out on any fun. They inherited simple pastimes; when the weather was moderate, they'd play *krenji*—drawing six squares on the sole asphalt street, hopping one-legged on them, one after the other, while nudging a stone from one square to the next, so that the stone wouldn't be stuck on the lines between the squares — or the houses, as they would call them.

When it was blistering hot or freezing cold, they'd go inside one of their homes to play *saglah*. They'd bring five dice, each one nothing more than a sheep's cartilage, rectangular-shaped, with four faces — two of them convex and the other two concave. They'd toss all five dice on the floor and start throwing one of them up above while grabbing another from the ground at the same time. Even though the dice were clean of every shred of meat and wiped down in chlorine, the smell of fat clung to their palms even after repeated washing. Their greatest enjoyment came during the summer nights when they'd be strewn in the alleys and on the rooftops like birds let loose from a cage, overcome with the desire to soar towards the beautiful sky as far away as possible from their impoverished quarter, their crumbling homes, with roofs still made out of poplar wood!

These pastimes didn't capture Leila's attention as much as the fence between her house and Sitt Najmiyyah's did: a fence enveloped by a frame of grapevines, whose clay-like nature the casual observer didn't cotton on to, a testament to the potter's skill. Since forever in this quarter, they've been jabbering about the story of Najmiyyah, daughter of the red djinn king. Najmiyyah, who one day surprised Mariam in her own house while Mariam was washing her children's diaper cloths and pouring the hot foul water down the bathroom drain. Everyone in the neighborhood swore that Mariam had seen Najmiyyah with her very own eyes and had spoken to her with her tongue, which the worms have since gobbled up. Najmiyyah was a real princess like the human princesses, but her palms and feet were lumps of flesh, no fingers or nails to speak of.

"You're a good woman, Mariam," Najmiyyah asserted. "I admire you and want to be your sister. I'm the only child of a king, no brothers or sisters to ease my loneliness, and in return for your sisterhood, I'll grant riches to you, your children, and your children's children. Here's the first of your gifts."

No sooner had Mariam, terrified, got a hold of her senses than clay jars full of golden coins piled up round her. Najmiyyah then disappeared, leaving Mariam shell-shocked.

After Mariam got a hold of herself, she decided not to touch the gold, and to not accept Najmiyyah's offer, fearful for her children, who would enter the world of the djinn, about which she had often heard terrifying tales. But her husband insisted on bringing a sheikh to the house. Surely he would provide them with a solution. Upon arrival, the cleric couldn't restrain himself in front of the jars of gold, and he ordered Mariam and her husband not to touch anything until reinforcements arrived. Meanwhile, the news had already spread, so the police arrived on the scene and arrested Mariam's family, claiming they had unearthed an archaeological treasure that belonged to the nation. Between the sheikh and the police, the gold was lost and Mariam's family left the house where only the djinn now lived, usurping a group of mud rooms surrounded by a plot in which pomegranates and olives grew in harmony with herbs and grasses, all possible only by divine decree.

Leila spent most of her days trying to get close to the fence, mustering the courage each night to take a step or two, only to return running to meet her family. Fear had burrowed a dark tunnel in her small heart.

Most of what happened in the neighborhood was attributed to the djinns of Sitt Najmiyyah's house. When someone fell ill, it was because the djinns were angry. If someone fell down, a djinn had pushed him, and if something went missing, a djinn had borrowed it and would return it soon. Even when one of the girls disappeared from the quarter, it was said that a djinn had fallen in love with her and kidnapped her because she refused to give in to him.

Leila was in even deeper, with her dreams and wishes tied to Sitt Najmiyyah's house. She would wait for the djinns to help her with her household chores and for them to bring her what her heart desired: games, sweets, clothes and other childish fancies. But something within her would refute these desires, especially when she heard her religious education teacher's words in school. Perhaps what troubled or terrified her even more was that she would be asked to go up to the roof to hang the laundry or collect it, or to overturn the tomato paste in the scattered pots under the sun. Things would only get worse at night. Compelled, she would go up, staying away from the wall as much as possible, turning her head in the other direction, then climb the ten steps as quickly as an arrow, snatching the laundry and coming down.

Leila realized that the passing of days in this manner wasn't rational and that she couldn't coexist with fear in one place at one time. When she searched for a solution, confrontation was the only one she found.

One night, she decided to go up. She didn't think about the break-in, only about what would come after. Either she would remain a coward or be a victor forever. She went up to the roof and approached the wall stealthily, quickly, as if running away from her fear. When the decisive make-or-break moment came, she put her hands on the fence, her feet heavy on the ground, reciting the surahs she had memorized, the shortest ones, seeking Allah's protection from the little devils, and when she opened her eyes . . . .

The moon lit up the place. She saw the deserted rooms, surrounded by trees bowed under the weight of their fruit, her gaze piercing through the broken glass windows. She didn't find any djinns cooking or washing or carrying out evil deeds. There was no one. And when she grew emboldened, she yelled with all her might, "Najmiyyah, come to me!" Nothing stirred. Leila spent the night watching for the djinn until the twittering of dawn. She descended from the roof quietly and walked confidently by the fence, and from that day on she was no longer scared to hang the laundry or inspect the apricot jam.

Leila was no longer interested in listening to grandmothers' tales. She no longer shared in the moments of her peers' fear and anticipation or felt that sweet safety from clinging to her beloved friend when children would scramble to the door of Sitt Najmiyyah's house with the intention of scaring one another. Now, when she lost something, she would spend ages looking for it. And when someone she knew was harmed, she would wrack her brains to find the real reason behind it.

Leila left the neighborhood and flew to a distant country to continue her education. The djinns had no hand in it. When she returned, Sitt Najmiyyah's house was just as it had been, its secrets the engine of the children's and adults' lives. She would stand for a while by the fence, and every night beg for Sitt Najmiyyah to show herself. Not to give her gold, but to bring back that sweet shiver that she had lost so long ago.

14

Gun License

Everyone was singing the banquet's praises. It had truly been a luxurious party, overflowing with the most sumptuous food and drink, crowded with guests. It had been hosted by a high-ranking police officer in the town. People knew how well-connected he was to the bigwigs and that this feast had been one round of many meant to strengthen their bond, but what they didn't know was that this occasion in particular was for the sake of his younger brother's gun license, his brother who yesterday had turned twenty-one. The banquet had cost him a pretty penny, but no worry, a gun was a necessity for his brother; a weapon meant respect.

As for the mayor, he was delighted with the luxurious ties brought over from Milan, and presented them as gifts to some officials, while hinting at having more of his own. So the older brother decided to gift him more than one tie, why not? A gun was a necessity for his brother; it meant protection.

And here he is taking a call from a security operative, who's thanking him for the fine drink that he had sent a while ago, inquiring if it's available in a store nearby, because he has searched tirelessly for it in the market, but hasn't been lucky enough to find it. So the older brother sends him more than one bottle of that fine drink, which he brought over from a neighboring city. He would give the security official even more, because such a matter required maintaining good relations with the officials, and a gun was a necessity for his brother; it meant prestige.

His friends didn't let him down. After all, he was valuable and his request was so straightforward. There's the license now in his hands, and the gun slung on his brother's waist; respect, protection, prestige!

The younger brother only used his licensed gun but once. It was when they disagreed over their inheritance. His younger brother brandished the weapon in his face. He pulled the trigger.

15

A Bed for the King's Daughter

"Once upon a time in the Bosra kingdom in the land of Syria, a fortune teller informed the king that his only daughter, whom he had lived his life for, would die on her twentieth birthday from a scorpion sting. So what else could the king do except demand that a bed suspended in mid-air be built for her, as high up as the most skillful builders could possibly make it . . . .

The man, tormented by his infatuation, decided not to follow the news, not to frequent the websites that published her stories and articles. He shut himself off to anything related to that woman writer whose presence haunted and seduced him. As for her — well, she'd steal into his dreams every night, chatting with him a while then retreating, leaving him to wrestle again in the morning with his desire to track her down, and, with the utmost difficulty, coming out victorious every day.

She would write tirelessly, having a firm grip on all forms of media: audio, written, online, with the hypothetical receiver in mind, only him, the man that had boycotted her . . . .

> *"The columns grew taller, towering, competing with the sky, and up there a bed of marble was fashioned to fit the princess, who had been raised up to it before the fated day . . . ."*

He no longer left the house so as to avoid stumbling over anything that belonged to her, no cafes, no markets, no restaurants, no evenings out or visits to exhibitions, to any place where they might come together in an anticipated or sudden coincidence. This made him a pioneer of unusual places in town, places that women's feet couldn't reach.

> *The king's daughter lay down peacefully in her bed. The servants would use a rope to send food and drink up to her. And in this way, everyone kept her from being injured. Her twentieth birthday passed by carefree. At the very end of it she received a basket of the choicest fruits to celebrate, except that the fated scorpion was hidden between the bunches of green grapes and stung her as soon as she reached out her hand, and she died."*

There, in a distant neighborhood that was located on the fringes of the city, he sat in the stillness of the evening to eat his food. Before he tossed away the torn-out magazine page wrapped around his hot sandwich, he read the story entitled *Bed of the King's Daughter*. At the very bottom was the name of the female writer he had been trying all along to avoid.

16

Wishing Tree

I had just finished decorating the Christmas tree, after a long day of tedious housework. I stood to the side, contemplating its splendor, yearning for joy, peace; recalling small and big dreams. After thirty years, it was still loaded with those shiny, hanging baubles that twinkled with the slightest movement, my wishes and hopes glistening along with them. At that moment my husband came in saying, "You've got half an hour to think of what you want for Christmas."

Since childhood, I was used to jotting down my wishes and the gifts I wanted on small colored pieces of paper, and then hanging them on the tree. I picked up a few scraps of colored paper while my husband repeated, on his way out, "Just half an hour!"

I turned my attention to writing when my daughter started crying behind me. I tried to ignore her, but her cries grew sharper, as if calling out for help. She had wet herself, and was hungry too, it seemed. I made my way to her.

Then I tried to start writing again, but as soon as I picked up the pen, the phone rang. I tried to ignore it, but it kept on ringing. I looked at the caller ID and recognized my dear friend's number. Picking up, I learned my friend had a dilemma and needed my advice. We chatted, she warmed to my point of view, and we promised to meet up soon.

Again I picked up the pen and one of the colored pieces of paper, and started to write. Suddenly the oven timer went off, which I couldn't ignore, otherwise I'd burn the Christmas cake.

Rushing to the kitchen, I removed the cake with somewhat-frayed oven gloves through which the heat of the baking tin burned my hands. Throwing the tin on the table any which way, I knocked over a container of oil onto the floor. I'd have to really scrub the floor to get the grease out.

My daughter's voice rang out from the other room; she was crying again. In all this commotion, my husband came home. After having thrown a glance at the tree, he said, completely straight-faced, "Seems like you don't want anything this year. Merry Christmas!"

After my husband had gone to bed, I put everything back in order and returned to the papers waiting for me. It seemed that the time — and I don't know how serious my husband was about it — was up. I actually only had one wish: that I'd have enough time to write this story down.

17

Greek Discussions

Habeas asked Socrates, "Isn't embellished armor splendid?"

"Of course, and I swear by Zeus it's beautiful. But it wouldn't be so if it were broken."

Habeas scowled. "What does its beauty have to do with it being broken?"

"Habeas, didn't I tell you that the beautiful is what is useful? Broken armor, however beautiful its design, won't protect the knight from his enemy's blows."

Habeas' wife trembled, joining in. "Of course, I swear by Zeus, what is useful is beautiful, but broken armor is also beautiful, because it keeps my husband in my arms."

18

Environmental Safety

The student who had come from a remote area, and who had been sent by the university to continue his studies in France, killed his lover. He had seen her in the company of a French man. French universities thereafter decided to request, in addition to the usual foreign student paperwork, a document from the home university attesting that the environment that the foreign student belonged to was a healthy one and prepared them to live in France.

Those in charge of this matter found themselves in a pickle, for even the most senior of them were unable to procure such a document from the country sending over their students. One man suggested that the Ministry of Education should furnish it. Another insisted the document fall under the Ministry of Agriculture's jurisdiction. And another chipped in his two cents, saying that the Ministry of Health should be the body taking this on . . . .

And so it came to pass that the foreign students received this document from the Meteorology Department until the Ministry of Environment came into being.

19

Lilith

What confused her was a man's desire to leave his wife and take a mistress. One day, a holy manuscript fell into her hands telling the tale of mankind. When she decoded it, she came to know that Adam had fallen in love with Lilith, and that he had asked her to lie down with him. She refused and ran away from him, leaving heaven behind. He continued to lament until God created Eve from his rib and married her to him. But his heart was still hung up on Lilith, and so he spent his nights dreaming of her lying down beside him.

And from that day onwards, the woman who had read the holy manuscript slept standing upright.

20

Kind Hearts

Fatigue weighed me down. The road
to my distant city was very long and,
being narrow and one-way, it frayed
my nerves. I wasn't able to stay up
with my parents even though I
hadn't seen them in a long time. As
soon as I flung my body onto the
bed, I fell into a deep sleep. I don't
know exactly how much I slept,
but I estimated from the darkness
cloaking the balcony in front of me
that I hadn't slept more than an hour
and that we were still in the second
third of the night. The voice that
woke me up was chilling and painful

at the same time: chilling because it was so late for such a racket, and painful because it was the moving voice of a heartbroken old man yelling, "Brothers, whoever finds a lost four-year-old girl, *please* bring her to Umar Bin Al-Khattab mosque and may God reward you!" Then he repeated, "Brothers, whoever finds a lost five-year-old girl, *please* bring her to the big mosque, for to God we belong and to Him we return . . . Brothers! . . . Brothers!"

His words were wracked with turmoil; he was off-kilter, really, because of this matter. He must have lost his daughter or his granddaughter tonight. He was repeating and repeating the plea in a quivering voice, cutting me to the core, making it impossible for me to go back to sleep. I had to do something!

In the bed next to mine, my husband had woken up. He was also shaken. While he absorbed the nature of what was being yelled, horrific images flashed through my mind. What if my daughter were this lost girl? What would happen to her? Death could take her, which would be the lesser evil, because some pervert could also find her, and how many rapes had we heard of, or the selling of body parts? Or she could end up in safe hands but far from her family. Or . . . or . . . .

I made up my mind to help, and his next call pierced my heart. My husband didn't even try to speak or change out of his pajamas. He followed me to search with the old man for this missing girl.

We didn't find him outside. He must have moved on to another neighborhood to spur its residents into action. We got into the car and started searching for her without a plan. We crossed the small town more than once over the course of the hour, all in vain. We came back, our hearts aching.

My sister let us in, surprised that we were out at such an hour. We asked her if she had heard the old man's cries. She opened her mouth and her roaring laughter took us by surprise. "How kindhearted you both are!" she said. "He's just a madman who roams the streets at night, saying the same thing over and over. Then he moves on. There's no lost girl, no lost boy. He's just lost his mind."

21

Successful Strikes

The first woman said, "He would always tackle me to the ground, I knew that he was physically stronger than me, but I would still feel a sense of defeat followed by pleasure, the pleasure of quarreling.

"I'd go right back to teasing him, I'd pull the hat from his head and toss it to the wind with a kick directed at his waist. He'd run behind me on the beach, I'd flee and give his leaps a chance to catch up to me. He'd catch me and then throw me to the ground. I was seven and he was nine.

"One summer passed, and another, then another, and he still threw me to the ground . . . .

"Then twenty summers passed and he didn't come back to the beach, he didn't even say goodbye.

"One summer he came back, a young girl clinging to his waist. He didn't say anything or pick a fight with me, and I didn't bait him. We didn't fight, but he still threw me on the ground!"

The second woman said, "He used to teach me painting. He'd hold my hand tenderly, explore the white page with it, drawing lines and shapes in different colors. Then, being the playful child I was, I pushed his hand away. The paper was disturbed as were the lines, the paints spilled over, and he grew agitated. He grabbed my hand roughly, and I yelled. He squeezed harder, I pulled away, he pulled back, his watch making my hand bleed, his ring, the edge of the paintbrush . . . .

"I was also seven or so when I got this scar on the back of my hand. The long time that passed prompted him to pick me up lightly, grip me tightly, squeeze me in his arms until I lost control over my body. With whatever power I had left, I pushed him. He grew agitated, released me, but took my hand hostage. He crushed it, I yelled, he squeezed harder, I tried to break free, his watch making my hand bleed, his ring . . . .

"Now I have two scars on the back of my hand, twenty years apart."

22

What Happened in the Wheat Field

"Oh... how I've missed him!" This is what she confessed to herself on the way, while everything around her was humming with desire: the river that peeked timidly from behind the hills to her right; the fields of wheat on her left; and the smooth asphalt path on which she drove her small car.

"Perhaps the flocks of migrating birds this evening are the reason for us growing closer together!" This is the opening sentence that she had been practicing, with which to begin her rendezvous . . . .

She turned onto the dirt road with ease, not paying attention to what was forbidden or permitted, as her long wait was now a feverish ball of haste.

She didn't know how she threw herself at the doorstep of the hut that she had dared to leave abruptly years ago, because of its owner's harshness or occasional indifference, and to which she had returned today to apologize. Why was the door shut unlike ever before?

She set off to the wheat field behind the hut, to their favorite spot, which had seen many tears, promises, and kisses . . . .

Joy overtook her when she saw him standing among the stalks. She tried to remain patient until she could reach the spot where he was standing. Questions pounded in her head. *What's he thinking wearing a coat in this heat? Isn't that his old coat that's been worn out forever? Why has he tied his keffiyeh round his face? He'd only do that to protect his eyes during the raging dust storms. He's still as strange and astonishing as ever, this love of mine, growing taller with age rather than shorter!*

Her agitation grew with every step she took towards him. Should she call out so he would turn and see her? Or should she come up from behind and surprise him by grabbing his hand or kissing him? Or cover his eyes with her hand so he'd have to guess?

He didn't move a muscle; he was simply contemplating the horizon before him while she was pricked by jealousy over the birds that had settled calmly on his shoulders. She was right behind him now, but she couldn't sense his breath; there was only the smell of nature.

Overwhelmed with fury, she pushed him with all the strength she could muster, and he plunged forth headlong. Before her feet lay a scarecrow that wore his old clothes.

Milton Keynes UK
Ingram Content Group UK Ltd.
UKHW012109230923
429161UK00019B/448